The Salty Sailor

story by
Kristopher King
illustration by
Rohland DeMoss
editing by
Ronnajean Tarantino Juhola
Published by
Kingkrist Media

2020
kingkristmedia.com
ISBN 978-1-735-2627-0-3

The sailor rolled over and sat up.

He spat sand from his mouth and wondered how it got there.

He quickly realized that he'd only been dreaming about his wife and child.

Disoriented, he scanned the massive expanse of ocean in front of him.

He remembered the terror of the storm.

Tears burned his eyes as he looked around at the flotsam on the beach; two jerrycans, a useless life raft, a medical kit.

Remembering the sinking ship frightened him.

Remembering the souls lost, his friends, made him angry.

The salty sailor raged.

Tears burned his tongue and dissolved on his hot breath as he pointed a shaky finger and hissed at the ocean

"You lay there calm and beguiling, but when I embark upon your wilderness you decide to rush to a tempest and try to devour me!

You've ruined my life! You've stranded me from my family and everything that I love!"

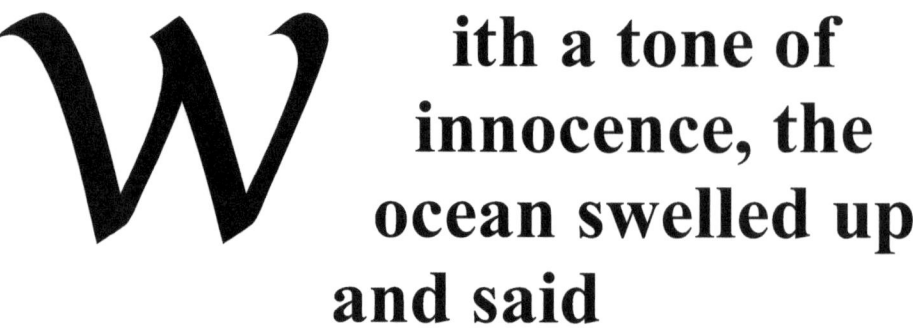

With a tone of innocence, the ocean swelled up and said

"My nature is calm, it is the wind that whips me into a frenzy.

The wind is the reason that I am this way!"

The wind whirled around the man, gently motioning towards the sky and whispered

"I am but air, without substance, only wanting to remain clear and steady.

It is the sun that disturbs me, with heat and fire.

It must be the sun to blame!"

T he sun burned his fiery eyes on the man and spoke flames

"I am pure energy. It is the great empty cold that disrupts my power!"

Pointing his wildfire into space, he proclaimed

"It is the fault of the stars!"

The stars gazed down at the man on the beach.

Silent and stoic they twinkled, flashing the ancient light and colors of eons past.

The man strained to look up into the glittery sum of everything.

The stars did not speak, but the salty sailor could hear them in his heart

"I am you. We are one. Oneness is not sameness, we are different by degrees, but like a wave to the ocean, a breeze to the wind, or fire to the sun, you are to me."

The sailor gaped at the heavens and heard the stars once more

"If we are not separate, then I have no one to blame. I must take ownership of every moment, good and bad, because I fall to earth in the hope of knowing love and pain, in the hope of solving problems old and new.

There are no obstacles in the cold darkness, so I fall into flesh and bone, I fall to be you."

Tears still burned the man's cheeks as they reflected the universe back upon itself, but this time they met a growing smile because he began to understand what was erupting in his heart.

The shame for blaming his problems on everything around him was giving way to gratitude for his new understanding.

After a silent moment the sailor raised his hands to the heavens and shouted

"Thank you!
Thank you for showing me who I am with every challenge I face!

Win or lose, I will forever strive to shine like the stars I am made of!"

Beaming, the Cosmos sprinkled its dust as it turned to the sun and spoke

"Thank you for your powerful light, so that we all may shine!"

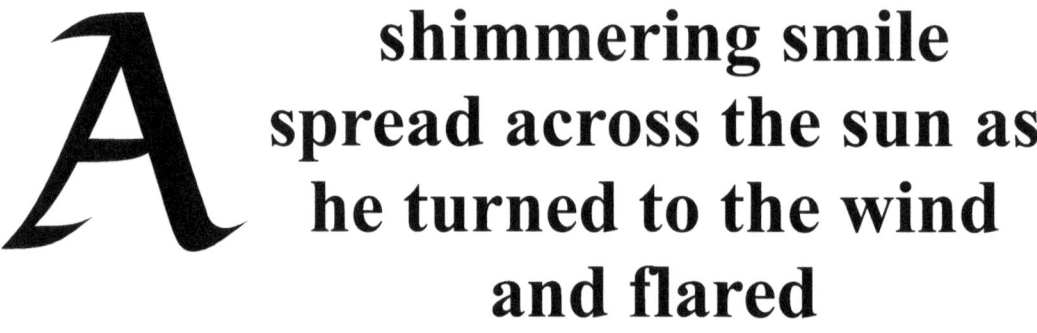

A shimmering smile spread across the sun as he turned to the wind and flared

"Thank you for your gentle breeze, keeping me from burning too hot and too powerful!"

The wind whirled in delight and glided across the surface of the ocean, fluttering

"Thank you mighty ocean. Your substance gives me strength!"

The ocean rolled with happiness.

A wave crashed on the shore and gathered around the man's feet, commingling with his tears and said

"Never forget what you've learned, and when you meet someone unkind or hurtful remember it is because they do not yet know.

We are all connected, there is no other way."

The sailor smiled. He gave a nod to the ocean, the wind, the sun, and the universe.

With his heart full of love and gratitude, he was ready to live with purpose, ready for all of life's challenges.

The man breathed deeply and looked again at his situation. He found the two jerrycans full of sweet water to quench his thirst. He noticed the life raft could be used for shelter. He also remembered that it stored enough food to keep him fed for weeks, along with rescue flares to signal a passing ship. He picked up the medical kit that contained plenty of first aid and he felt safe.

A ppreciating his good
fortune,
he began to plan for
his survival.

Looking into the distance he
noticed the faint outline of a
ship heading his way.

www.ingramcontent.com/pod-product-compliance
Lightning Source LLC
Chambersburg PA
CBHW041012170626
46815CB00003B/271